Howard M. Chapin

How to Enamel; Being a Treatise on the Practical Enameling of Jewelry with Hard Enamels

in large print

 MEGALI

Howard M. Chapin

How to Enamel; Being a Treatise on the Practical Enameling of Jewelry with Hard Enamels

in large print

Reproduction of the original.

1st Edition 2023 | ISBN: 978-3-38708-470-2

Megali Verlag is an imprint of Outlook Verlagsgesellschaft mbH.

Verlag (Publisher): Outlook Verlag GmbH, Zeilweg 44, 60439 Frankfurt, Deutschland
Vertretungsberechtigt (Authorized to represent): E. Roepke, Zeilweg 44, 60439 Frankfurt, Deutschland
Druck (Print): Books on Demand GmbH, In de Tarpen 42, 22848 Norderstedt, Deutschland

HOW TO ENAMEL

BEING A TREATISE ON THE PRACTICAL ENAMELING OF JEWELRY WITH HARD ENAMELS

BY

HOWARD M. CHAPIN

1911

PREFACE

The aim of this book is to explain practical enameling in such a way that one entirely unacquainted with the subject will, after a little study, not only understand the fundamental principles of the art, but with a little practice be able actually to achieve creditable results in this most fascinating branch of the jeweler's craft.

INTRODUCTION

Enamel is really a glaze applied to metals just as other glazes are applied to porcelain, glass, and earthenware. We will confine our attention to what is known as hard enamel in contradistinction to japans, lacquers, and enamel paints, which are often called soft enamels. Hard enamels are compounds of glass with different metallic oxides which produce the different colors. These compounds are fused together at a very high temperature and on cooling become extremely hard. They fill the gap between glass and china, the transparent fondants being to the layman indistinguishable from glass, while the opaque whites may be easily mistaken for china, and the countless other varieties form a chain of scarcely perceptible gradations from one extreme to the other.

Fig. 1. Agate Mortar and Pestle.

The use of enamels is both very ancient and very widespread, for we find the process known to the ancient Egyptians and to the Chinese, although the highest development in the art was reached in France in the sixteenth century. We would refer the historical student to Cunynghame's "European Enamels" in English and Luthmer's "Enamel" in German.

Jewelry enameling is usually divided into five different classes, viz: champlevé, cloisonné, incrusted, plique-à-jour, and enamel painting.

Champlevé enamel is that in which a part of the metal is cut away, leaving a depression which is filled with enamel to the level of the surface of the metal, thus giving a sort of inlaid effect. If the enamel surface is not filed off flat but allowed to have a concave or convex surface the piece is said to be "flushed." Technically enamel is "flushed" if it is not "stoned." When transparent enamels are used and the background under the enamel is cut in relief, it is called "Baisse-taille enamel."

Cloisonné enamel is hardly distinguishable from champlevé when finished, but is made differently. Instead of cutting depressions in the metal to hold the enamel, metal wires are soldered on the smooth surface of the metal, thus forming partitions or fences between which the enamel is placed.

Incrusted enamel is that in which the enamel is charged directly on the metal surface without any raised metal edges to hold it. It is generally used in small daubs or beads to reproduce the effect of precious stones.

Plique-à-jour enamel is similar to cloisonné except that the wires are soldered to each other without any background, thus forming a sort of filigree, the spaces within which, when filled with enamel, somewhat resemble a stained-glass window.

In enamel painting a picture is painted on the enamel. Usually white opaque enamel is used for the background, and the painting is executed with finely ground enamel or china paints, after which it is covered with a layer of transparent enamel which serves as a protection for the painting.

CHAPTER I

PREPARATION OF THE ENAMELS

ENAMEL is generally bought in the form of hard chunks more or less flat and varying from the size of an acorn to that of a large dinner plate. When it is made it is poured into a mold where it hardens in the form of a disk or slab generally a foot or more in diameter, and later gets broken into smaller pieces during transportation.

These chunks of enamel may be readily broken up by a hammer, and if they are first wrapped in a piece of cloth the small particles will not fly about and get into one's eye, and no enamel will be lost. When the enamel has been broken up so that none of the pieces are larger than a pea, it should be washed in clean water to free it from any dirt that it naturally contained or that it received from the cloth in which it was wrapped during the hammering process.

Cleanliness cannot be too much emphasized, for the slightest particle of dirt mixed in with the enamel may often completely spoil a piece of work.

Enamel if heated quite hot and then plunged into cold water will become so brittle that it can be broken up by the hands, but when treated in this manner is said to be harder to grind.

6

Fig. 2. Grinding with Weighted Pestle.

After the enamel has been broken up into small pieces it should be put in an agate or porcelain mortar and ground to a fine powder. This will take from twenty to twenty-five minutes of steady grinding, the length of time depending on the quality and quantity of the enamel, the strength used, etc. Water may or may not be mixed with the enamel during the grinding process, as the grinder prefers. If water is added the process may take a little longer but a very disagreeable noise is eliminated and the work may perhaps be slightly easier. Agate mortars are cleaner and so better than porcelain ones but are so much more expensive that they cannot be used for grinding large amounts. For this grinding machines or weighted pestles, such as Cunynghame describes in his "Art Enameling upon Metals," should be used. The enamel should be ground until it is about the size of fine sand, and soft, not gritty, when rubbed gently between one's thumb and forefinger. It should now be rinsed in clean (the purer the better) running water, the enamel being thoroughly stirred up and washed, the fine particles, "dregs" or "slimes" as they are called, being allowed to flow away. Often from ten to thirty per cent of the enamel is lost in this process. The remaining wet enamel powder is ready to be used. It may be kept for weeks under water in a glass jar or druggist's salve box, but in time is said to deteriorate. If the enamel is to be used immediately it may be placed upon a clean copper or china palette which will be found very serviceable. It should be kept constantly wet and if possible under water. If, however, it becomes dry, it may be washed as described above and will probably be found in good condition; if not a slight grinding may assist matters.

If enamel is not ground fine enough it is apt to have pit-holes in it when fired, and if it is not absolutely clean it is likely to have both pit-holes and black spots in it. Sometimes enamel is washed in nitric acid as well as water but this is generally not necessary. It is very important, however, to use water that contains very little iron, for iron will cause black spots in the enamel.

If enamel is to be kept for any length of time it should be kept either as chunks preferably or as coarsely ground powder. When coarsely ground it may be kept dry in a dirt-proof jar or bottle.

The "dregs" and "slimes" if washed clean may be kept and used for paints in painting on enamel.

When enamel is bought in the form of a powder it is generally necessary to grind it finer and wash it thoroughly.

CHAPTER II

PREPARATION OF THE METALS

MANY metals can be enameled, but the most practical ones, those most used in jewelry, are gold, silver, copper, and their alloys. Hence we will confine our descriptions to these metals.

Whatever metal is used, however, must first be made chemically clean before it is "charged" or covered with enamel. This may be done in a number of different ways, of which the following is considered the most practical.

The metal, whether gold, silver, or copper, must be annealed by being heated to a red heat and allowed to cool slowly in the air. When cool it will be found to be covered with a black oxide.

The metal must now be plunged for half a minute or more into a solution called a "dip," consisting of two parts sulphuric acid (H_2SO_4), two parts nitric acid (HNO_3), and a slight touch of hydrochloric acid (HCl); a few drops of the latter to the gallon will suffice. This dip will clean the surface of the metal and make it bright. As the solution gets old it will become weak and a longer dip will be required. The ordinary commercial acids are suitable for making these dips. Care should be taken not to inhale the fumes of the acids, as they are quite poisonous.

This dip may be used cold, but better results are obtained when it is heated to 170°F. A convenient way to heat it is to set the jar containing the dip in a larger jar containing water and then to heat the water in the larger jar.

Many prefer to use first a hot and then a cold dip, rinsing the metal in clean water between the dips. Experience will soon teach one to tell when the metal is clean by looking at it, and this in fact is the only satisfactory way, as the length of time required will vary with the condition of the metals and the strength of the dip.

Fig. 3. Enameler's Spatula with Wooden Handle.

After the dip the metal must be thoroughly rinsed in clean water and then dried in clean sawdust or hot air. If rinsed in very hot water the metal will dry itself almost immediately. Some prefer to rinse the metal in ammonia as well as in water in order to rid it of all trace of the acid, but this is not generally necessary. If the metal is copper or gold it is now ready to be charged, but if it is silver it must be "fire-stained."

There are many other possible ways of cleaning metals, but the above means are generally used and will doubtless be found the most convenient. If small quantities only are being "cleaned," a copper pickle pan and a Bunsen gas burner will suffice, while for large quantities earthen pickle pots and large jars will be found advantageous. Metals if "wriggled," that is, scraped or engraved all over with a graver, are generally clean enough to be charged.

If silver is used it must be "fire-stained," or have the "fire" taken out of it. This is done in the following manner. The silver is submerged for a minute or more in a solution of four parts nitric acid and one part water, heated to 170°F. The acid will react on the silver, which will become covered with a brownish scum. The silver should now be rinsed in clean water and brushed with a metal brush in a solution of soap-tree bark and water. This will clean the scum off the silver and make the latter bright. After being rinsed in clean water, the silver is ready to be charged with enamel. Sour beer, or a solution of licorice root and water may be used instead of soap-tree bark. It will be very convenient to have the metal wire brush a circular one revolving on a lathe.

If red enamel is to be used, the metal should always be either wriggled or engine turned or else have some design cut sharply in it, in order to bring out the brilliancy of the color. Engine turning and sharp engraving or relief in the metal background will always enhance the brilliancy and give an additional sheen to any transparent colors. As the

11

depth of the enamel layer has a great deal to do with the shade of the enamel, different effects can be obtained, even when only one enamel is used, if the metal background has been cut lower in some places than in others.

If the silver is not "fire-stained," red enamel will often become maroon when fired, and fondant and other delicate colors will become streaked or spotted. If the fire-staining and dipping have not been carefully done, the enamel is likely to chip out, have pit-holes in it, or contain black blotches.

As the acid fumes eat the flesh quite rapidly, it is advisable to wear rubber gloves when dipping the metals.

CHAPTER III

CHARGING

ENAMEL is "charged," or put on the metal, in the form of a watery mud, by means of a small spatula. The most convenient spatula is one made from a piece of steel wire about the size of a crochet needle and flattened at one end. In fact a crochet needle itself, flattened at one end, or even the small blade of a penknife, will be found quite serviceable. If this spatula is mounted in a wooden handle made from a penholder it will be found very easy to handle.

Fig. 4. Charging.

A small daub of very watery enamel should be taken on the end of the spatula and laid upon the metal where it is to be enameled. If the surface to be enameled is very large, a larger spatula can be used to advantage. If the enamel is too watery it will not stick to the spatula while being taken from the palette, and if it is too dry it cannot be readily transferred from the spatula to the metal.

When the piece has been entirely covered with enamel, it should be held in the hand and tapped gently with the spatula. If the enamel is wet enough this procedure will spread it evenly over the metal. The water should now be drawn off from the enamel by means of a clean piece of cloth or blotting paper. The remaining moisture will soon evaporate, leaving the enamel perfectly dry. Only when perfectly dry is it in a condition to be fired.

Care must be taken not to get the enamel on too thick, as in that case it will chip off when fired. On the other hand, enamel shrinks considerably on being fired, so if it is put on too thin it is apt to shrink, leaving bare spaces of metal. The proper thickness with which to charge a piece of work can only be learned by experiment, and in most cases it is desirable to charge a piece with several thin coats rather than with one thick one.

In cloisonné and champlevé work it is generally necessary to use at least two coats in order to bring the enamel up to the level of the metal parts. Originally in these kinds of enameling the idea was to have each color or shade of enamel separated by a metal wall from every other shade, which made the charging comparatively simple. Now the vulgar modern taste permits several different shades side by side without partitions, or even blended. If the enamel is not too wet two distinct colors can be charged side by side without having them run into each other to any appreciable extent. They may then be fired, and they will be no more mixed in that process than they were before it.

A blend between two colors may be obtained by mixing two enamels together and then charging the piece with the mixture. Such a mixture when fired is often found to be speckled instead of a clear shade. If, after mixing, the enamel is ground finer, this speckled effect can sometimes be eliminated. This process is by no means always satisfactory.

Another way that two colors can be blended is as follows: Divide a piece to be enameled into three parts by two imaginary lines and call the parts *A*, *B*, and *C*. Now charge *A* and *B* with a thin coat of, for instance, blue, and *C* with a thin coat of red, and fire the piece. Then on the second charging charge *A* with blue and *B* and *C* with red. When fired, part *B* will be found intermediate between *A* and *C*, in this case a sort of purple. This purple may be made bluish or reddish, as desired, by using a preponderance of blue or of red enamel. This preponderance can be largely regulated by the thickness of the layers or coats of each color, although the last coat, other things being equal, will, on account of its position, exert by far the stronger influence.

With most transparent colors it is desirable, though not necessary except in the case of so-called "opals," to use an under layer of fondant, that is, on the first charging, to cover the entire surface with a thin layer of transparent white or colorless enamel, commonly called flux or fondant. This under layer of fondant is used more on gold than on silver or copper, but in any case it will greatly enhance the brilliancy of the enamels. It is of great assistance in bringing out delicate colors and especially "opals," for if opals are charged directly upon the stock they have a strong tendency to become opaque when fired. Some delicate roses and pinks if put directly upon the metal will "fire" black, while over a layer of fondant they became beautiful and delicate shades.

Where several colors are used on the same piece it is generally advantageous to use fondant for the last layer. The advantage of this is that the harmony and qualities of the different colors are then not affected by the stoning and polishing, which no matter how carefully done are bound to cut down the enamel, and in the case of transparent colors the thinner a layer becomes the lighter it becomes.

Any transparent color can be made lighter either by being stoned down or by being put on over a layer of fondant. Transparent white can easily be obtained on silver by the use of bluish and white fondants, but it is impossible to obtain transparent white on gold or copper unless these metals are first plated with silver.

Most enamels appear to best advantage on silver over fondant, and when the same enamel is put on another metal it changes its hue. This change of hue varies with each individual enamel and can only be learned by experiment. In general, white (fondant) on silver becomes pink on gold or copper, orange becomes red, yellow becomes orange or brown, blue has a tendency to green and green to yellow. Opaque colors of course do not actually change color, but owing to the different color of their setting they often give different effects.

Some shades that cannot be obtained by mechanically mixing opaque colors or by layers of different transparent colors, can be obtained by putting a layer of transparent enamel over a layer of opaque. Opaque white as an under layer will often give a desirable shade to a transparent enamel which is not just the color required.

16

CHAPTER IV

FIRING

AFTER enamel has been charged on a piece of metal, it is "fired," that is, heated until the enamel is fused, after which, on cooling, it becomes hard. It is best fired in a muffle furnace, although with care a nice job may be done with a blowpipe, a Bunsen burner, or even an alcohol lamp.

In case a Bunsen burner or lamp is used, it is well to have a metal tripod supporting a sheet of metal or wire mesh on which to set the work, as holding it by a pair of tongs becomes very tedious.

Fig. 5. Metal Tray or Tile.

A muffle may be heated by electricity, gas (with or without an air blast), oil, coal, or wood. Electricity or gas, however, is preferable, as they are not accompanied by dirt. The muffle itself, which is simply a small oven, is generally made of fire clay, although both fused quartz and nickel are sometimes used. A door to the muffle is not necessary, although it is an aid to cleanliness. If, however, a door is used it should have a hole in it large enough to allow the enameler to watch his work constantly. It is very important to keep the enamel work away from the oxidizing effect of the fire; so that any cracks that appear in a muffle must be immediately repaired. It will be found very advantageous, too, to have the doors of the furnace on the side of it opposite to that containing the mouth of the muffle.

The pieces to be fired should be laid upon a tray of a size convenient to pass easily through the mouth of the muffle. These trays are made preferably of sheet nickel for this metal will not scale or flake off when heated and so contaminate the enamel. As these trays become quite hot it is advisable to handle them by means of a pair of long-handled tongs.

Before placing a tray of pieces in the muffle to be fired, it is well to leave it near the mouth of the muffle for a minute or two so that the enamel may become entirely dry before it is placed in the muffle, for if damp the enamel will be blown off of the metal by the rapid evaporation of the water which it contains.

When the pieces are fully dry, the tray may be placed in the muffle, which should be heated to a bright red heat of about 1400° F. With such a heat it should take from half a minute to two minutes to "fire" or melt the enamel. The time required will vary with different enamels and can only be learned by experiment. The enamel should be kept in the muffle until it begins to melt and its surface becomes fused and comparatively smooth and glossy, when it should be

18

removed from the furnace and allowed to cool in the air. It is not necessary or even desirable to fire the enamel perfectly smooth in the first firing. It generally takes at least two coats, that is two chargings and two firings, before a piece is ready to be stoned. If, however, only one coat is to be used, it should be fired as smooth as possible.

When the pieces cool, the metal (unless it is fine, *i.e.*, pure, unalloyed) will be found covered with a black scale caused by oxidation. This may be removed by simply brushing it, which operation in most cases will clean the piece sufficiently for the second charging. Otherwise the piece may be "pickled," or cleaned with acid.

Subsequent firings do not differ from the first one except that in the last firing the enameler should try to obtain as smooth a surface as possible.

After the last firing the pieces should be submerged for a minute or two in a mild pickle consisting of one part sulphuric acid and one part water. This will clean off the oxide and make the metal bright.

If red enamel is used it is best to throw the piece into a cup of thick heavy machine oil to cool instead of letting it cool in the air. This will give the red a greater brilliancy. Red enamel, too, often requires a greater heat than other colors, although too low a heat tends to destroy the gloss on any enamel. Many delicate colors which are opaque when fired at a low heat, will become opalescent and in some cases transparent if fired at a higher temperature. Red enamel loses its color if fired too many times, and a large number of firings have a weakening effect on high-karat gold.

CHAPTER V

STONING

AFTER a piece of enamel has been fired, it is often found that too much enamel has been used, that is, that the enamel may have run over the edge of the part to be enameled, or it may not present a smooth surface but instead consist of a series of humps, or, especially in the case of transparent enamels, it may be on in such layers that the color is deepened or even lost entirely.

This can be remedied by what is known as "stoning," or filing the enamel down to a smooth surface. In the case of work that is to be polished it is always considered best to overcharge the piece and then file it smooth rather than to try to "flush" it evenly.

Stoning is usually done by means of emery "stones" or "sticks," which are made by mixing powdered emery with shellac and heating the same until the mixture coheres, when it may be pressed into any shape desired by means of a flat piece of steel. On cooling the stones become very hard. They are generally from six to twelve inches long and from three-eighths to one inch square, tapering at both ends to a rather blunt point. When a stone wears out or loses its shape it can be remelted and remodeled. The emery used in these sticks runs from No. 70 to No. 180 grit.

Fig. 6. Firing.

Carborundum stones are often used in place of emery stones. They are rather more expensive than emery stones and wear out quicker, but they cut the work down much faster. No. 120 and No. 180 grits are the most satisfactory. These stones sometimes get filled up with metal, but in this case the metal can be eaten out with acid.

It is convenient when stoning to hold the piece to be stoned on a small block of wood, on which a mold of shellac has been made into which mold the piece of work will snugly fit. If the block is then set on a pivot either on a bench or bench-pin, so that it will turn easily, it will then be found that the stoning process has been made considerably easier. A piece of hard felt or leather or just a plain piece of wood will, however, answer the purpose. The idea is simply to hold the piece firmly and conveniently.

The stone should now be rubbed back and forth across the enamel as a file is used. It is necessary when stoning to keep both the stone and the piece to be stoned quite wet. A bowl full of water kept near by will be found very convenient for the purpose. Care must be taken not to make any deep scratches on the metallic parts of the piece, as these scratches cannot easily be obliterated.

The stoning should be continued until the surface is smooth or level with the edges, or until in champlevé and cloisonné enamel the metal parts all show evenly, or until the desired depths of color are obtained in the case of transparent enamels. This of course can only be judged by experience, as the colors will look much brighter when fired again.

When the stoning is finished it will be found that the surface of the enamel presents a rather dull or dead appearance, which will be removed by again firing the piece. Before this firing, however, the piece should be submerged for about a minute or less in hydrofluoric acid and then brushed in clean water. This may be done with any small stiff-bristled hand brush. The piece will dry readily in the air, but more quickly if first dipped in scalding hot water or brought in contact with steam. It may also be dried in hot air or sawdust. When dry it is ready to be fired.

Sometimes after stoning, low places or pit-holes are found in the enamel surface, which may be remedied by re-charging these places with enamel and then firing the piece.

When only a very small amount of enamel is to be stoned off, or when one does not want to fire the piece after the stoning, a soft soapstone called a "Scotch stone" may be used to advantage.

If the piece to be stoned is small it is desirable to have a small wooden stick the size of a pencil with which to hold the piece steady and keep it from slipping out of its mold. Of course a mold is not always necessary, but will often be found very convenient.

A sharp steel tool, such as a three-cornered scraper or a slightly dull awl, is very useful to clean out pit-holes or to chip enamel off from places where it is not desired.

When a large number of pieces are to be stoned, it is advantageous to use an emery or carborundum wheel of No. 90 to No. 120 grit, from two and one-half to six inches in diameter and from three-eighths to three-fourths of an inch thick, revolving on a lathe at a low rate of speed. A stream of water should be kept constantly dropping on the wheel in order to keep both the wheel and the work wet.

Rubber cots are a great protection to the fingers, which are gradually worn away by the stones.

CHAPTER VI

POLISHING

AFTER an enameled piece has been stoned and fired for the last time, it is often desirable to give the enamel a gloss or polish additional to that which it naturally receives from the firing.

Fig. 7. Carborundum or Emery Stone.

If the metal used is other than fine gold or fine silver it will be black or oxidized when taken from the furnace, in which case it should be "pickled," that is, submerged for a minute or two, until the oxidization is removed and the metal becomes bright, in a mild "pickle" consisting of a warm solution of one part sulphuric acid and one part water. The piece should now be rinsed in clean water, after which it will be ready to be polished.

Polishing is best done on a lathe with a swiftly revolving wheel, say about 2200 revolutions per minute. A wheel of from three to six inches in diameter, made of hard felt or wood, is very satisfactory. If the felt is thin it is often necessary to make a wooden back for it in order to keep it flat.

The piece to be polished should be held on a small piece of leather or felt so that the hands may not come in contact with the wheel, in which case the skin and nails would soon be worn away. Rubber finger cots will serve as an additional protection.

The enamel surface to be polished should first be covered with wet pumice of about the consistency of mud. Then the pumice-covered surface should be pressed against the face of the felt or wood wheel, and as soon as the pumice is removed by the action of the wheel more wet pumice-mud should be added so that the enamel surface may constantly be kept covered with wet pumice.

It is best to use the finest ground pumice obtainable, although on rough jobs a coarse grade may be used. Tutty powder (oxide of zinc) is said to give even a better polish than fine pumice, and is often used after a preliminary polish has been given by pumice. A different wheel should be used for each polishing compound.

The polishing should be kept up until the enamel surface takes on the desired gloss. This polishing process will cut away the metal quicker than it does the enamel, so that any slight lines and scratches which the metal received in the stoning will be removed by the polishing. Care must be taken not to polish away too much of the metal, or to cut down and destroy any metal ornaments which may be near the enameled part of the piece. Felt wheels being more pliable than wood wheels have a tendency to cut down the metal faster than they cut down the enamel (the enamel being harder than the metal), while wood wheels tend to cut down both parts equally. Felt wheels, however, are considered to give a better and quicker polish.

When the piece is polished sufficiently, it should be rinsed and brushed off in clean water, which will remove all trace of the pumice. The piece is now finished as far as the enameling process is concerned, but may, however, be plated, set with stones, engraved, etc., as may be desired.

If after the piece is polished it is found that there are a number of small pit-holes in it, in which the pumice sticks even after the brushing, this may be remedied by digging the pumice out with a scraper or any sharp instrument. If the hole is small and the enamel transparent it will scarcely show when clean owing to the refractive power of the enamel. If, however, the hole is so large and noticeable as to be objectionable it will have to be re-charged and re-fired. In such a case it is often possible after the first firing to stone it smooth with a Scotch stone or by polishing and thus avoid another firing.

CHAPTER VII

FOILS—PAILLONS—GLITTER ENAMEL—DULL FINISH—PLIQUE-À-JOUR

FOILS and paillons are generally made of fine gold or fine silver leaf. Silver foils are used on copper and gold work in order to obtain better enamel effects, for most transparent colors are shown to best advantage over silver. Gold foils are sometimes used on copper for similar reasons.

The metal is first charged and fired with a coat of any enamel, preferably a "hard running" white, that is, one that it takes a comparatively high temperature to melt. The foil is then stuck to the enamel by means of gum arabic, tragacanth or, in fact, some kinds of common mucilage will answer the purpose. As Cunynghame says, "What is wanted is a good tenacious gum, which disappears as completely as possible when heated and leaves no carbonaceous residue to spoil the enamel." The foil should be cut so that it will exactly fit the enamel surface, and cover it entirely so that none of the white enamel will show on the finished piece. If the foil is stamped with some design it will add greatly to the brilliancy of the enamel afterwards applied, and if it is pierced with a number of small holes through which the fumes of the gum can escape, it will stick smoothly to the enamel.

After the foil has been put upon the enamel, the piece should be fired until the foil adheres strongly and smoothly to the enamel, when it is ready for the next charging. From this point on the process does not differ from that employed when charging directly upon the metal. (See chapter on charging.)

Paillons are simply small bits of foil cut into dainty and artistic shapes such as stars, fleurs-de-lis, etc. They are applied by means of gum, as in the case of foils, on the surface of the last or upper layer of colored enamel, after it has been fired, and the piece is again fired, making the paillons adhere to the enamel. The piece is then charged all over with a coat of fondant and fired, after which it is ready to be stoned and polished, if desired.

Fig. 8. Stoning.

Glitter enamel, called by the Germans "flimmer," is simply ground up goldstone (Aventurin) mixed with an ordinary enamel in equal proportions or two parts of goldstone to one of enamel. Some very striking effects can be produced with this mixture, which should be stoned to bring out the brilliancy of the goldstone. The best effects are obtained when some dark opaque enamel is used.

To obtain the so-called dead or dull finish on enameled goods, it is only necessary to submerge the piece for two or three minutes in a solution of hydrofluoric acid. This will "etch" the enamel leaving the surface dull like ground glass. When the piece is etched evenly all over, it should be removed from the acid and washed and dried. The etching will only take a few minutes if the acid is strong, and will be done much more evenly if a mixture of hydrofluoric acid and ammonium carbonate, known as white acid, is used.

If only part of the surface is to be dulled or etched, the part that is not to be etched should be covered with shellac, or a mixture of three parts beeswax and one part Burgundy pitch, and allowed to dry before the piece is put in the acid. The acid must be kept either in lead or wax bottles, as it eats glass very rapidly. Its fumes are very dangerous and destroy human tissues.

If for some reason a piece has been enameled wrong, so that it is desirable to take the enamel off the metal, this can best be done by leaving the piece for a few hours in a solution of hydrofluoric acid which will eat the enamel, so that it can easily be brushed off the metal, leaving it bright.

Plique-à-jour enamel may be done in several ways. The simplest is to lay the filigree work upon a piece of mica or fire clay and charge with enamel, as if the mica or fire clay were the background and the filigree work the sides of the piece. The process continues the same as in ordinary enameling, except that just before the last firing the mica or fire clay should be removed.

Copper or silver foil may be used instead of mica, but in this case the filigree work must be either of gold or platinum, for the copper or silver foil can only be removed by being dissolved in nitric acid.

The most difficult way is to mix a little gum arabic or gum tragacanth with very finely ground enamel and charge a layer on the inner sides of the wires which make up the filigree work. The gums will hold the enamel in place after it is dried. When the piece has been fired, another layer of enamel should be charged and so on, until by degrees the entire space between the wires has been filled up. This process is tedious and requires much skill and care, but gives very satisfactory results.

CHAPTER VIII

ENAMEL PAINTING

ENAMEL painting is usually done on a background of opaque white enamel, although other opaque colors are sometimes used. The metal must be prepared in the regular manner, and one or two coats of enamel charged and fired, the last coat being fired to as perfect smoothness as possible. Instead of flushing the enamel smooth it is often advisable to stone and fire it, by which processes a smoother surface is obtained.

After this last firing, the black flakes of metallic oxide which will be found on the metal should be brushed away, leaving the piece clean and ready to be painted. It is desirable not to have too thick a layer of enamel, as in that case it is apt to chip off in some of the later firings. If, on the other hand, the enamel layer is thin, it is quite difficult to get it smooth.

Fig. 9. Copper Pickle Pan.

Any picture desired may now be painted on the enamel surface, either with ordinary china paints or finely ground enamel "slimes" mixed with oil of cloves or oil of lavender. This painting may be done with a small camel's-hair brush and when finished should be fired until the enamel fuses. The piece should be allowed to cool slowly and when cool should be charged with a coat or two of clear fondant which, after being fired, may or may not be stoned and polished, as the artist sees fit. If the painting requires it, it may be touched up and fired several times before being charged with the fondant, but the fewer times a piece is fired the less chance there is for accidents which may prove fatal to the work of art.

If the metal used is very thin, it will be necessary to enamel it on the back as well as on the front, for a thin piece of metal which is enameled on one side only will warp out of shape, but if enameled on both sides will keep its shape perfectly. Of course the enamel on the back may be of any color and need not be finished carefully, as it is there for use not ornament.

An enamel painting must be fired with great care. First it must be warmed by degrees before put into the muffle, so that the oil may have a chance to evaporate. It should then be placed partly in the muffle and not put way in and should not be heated to a red heat until the residues of the oils shall have burnt away. If too hot a muffle is used, or if the piece is fired too long, the painting will appear blurred and faint. If the painting appears blistered after firing, it is due to the fact that the oils used contained too much carbonaceous residue.

The fondant used on an enamel painting should be very finely ground, much more so than for ordinary work, and the first layer of fondant should not be fired to smoothness but only until it just begins to flow, as was the case with the painting itself. The last layer of fondant should of course be fired as smooth as possible.

If a large number of pieces are to be painted with the same design, there are a number of mechanical means that can be used to take the place of free-hand painting. We will outline one of these processes, which is as follows.

Etch a copper plate with the outline of the design that is to be painted on the enamel. The etching on the copper plate must be a positive, not a negative; that is, the design must appear on the plate as it is to appear on the enamel and not reversed as in ordinary etching. The design must also be exactly the same size as the one to appear on the enamel.

The lines in the etching should now be filled with finely ground enamel paints mixed with oil of cloves or some such medium. It is best to use paint of the color that is to predominate in the picture, although in some cases it will be found that black will give the best working outline.

When the lines of the etching are filled with the paint, the plate should be scraped smooth so that no paint remains on it except in the etched lines. The plate should now be pressed against a piece of thin, smooth, sheet rubber, to which the paint will stick in preference to the copper plate, thus transferring the design to the sheet of rubber, where it appears reversed.

The rubber with the design side down is now pressed upon the smooth surface of the white enamel, which should be prepared in the same way as it would be prepared for regular painting. The design is thus transferred from the rubber to the enamel surface, where it appears again positive.

The enamel surface now has on it the outline of the design either in black or in color as the case may be. From this point on, the process is the same as in regular hand painting on enamel, but as the outline has been blocked in, the work is considerably easier. A speed and uniformity are obtained by this process which it is difficult to equal with free-hand work.

Another process whereby a number of similar designs can be easily executed is by decalcomania. Decalcomania pictures are made in Germany and can be obtained through any artists' supply house. In this case the white enamel background is obtained in the usual manner, after which a decalcomania picture is transferred to the enamel surface. The enamel is first covered with a very thin layer of size or gum as in the case of foils. When the size becomes sticky, the decalcomania picture should be placed face downwards on the enamel. The paper on the back of the picture should now be wet with a sponge until it becomes loose, when it should be removed and the remaining scum washed off with plenty of clean water. The piece after being dried thoroughly is ready to be fired. The rest of the process is the same as in regular painted enamel work. Great care must be taken in firing the decalcomania work.

CHAPTER IX

PHOTOGRAPHS ON ENAMEL

THERE are several methods by which photographs may be reproduced upon enamel. However, since they are rather difficult, we will explain only one method, and for the other processes will refer the student to Dr. Paul Liesegang's treatise on photographing on enamel, porcelain, and glass, which is printed in German.

In the first place only the best quality of mirror glass should be used for the plates, as it is essential that they should be perfectly smooth and without blemishes. The glass should then be cut the same size as the negative plate which is to be used later. The glass plate must be made perfectly clean, which is best done by placing it in a mild sulphuric acid bath for about ten minutes and then washing it well with clean water. It should be dried with a clean cloth or tissue paper, after which it may be wrapped in clean dry tissue paper and kept in a dry place until needed.

Fig. 10. Polishing.

Out of the many receipts for preparing the sensitive solution, we will give only the two most generally found satisfactory. These are as follows:

(1) Dissolve one-half ounce of ammonium bichromate in five ounces of clean water. In another glass dissolve one ounce of grape sugar and one ounce of gum arabic in five ounces of clean water. When the solutions are completely dissolved, they should be mixed together, stirred considerably, and filtered several times.

(2) Dissolve one-half ounce of Le Page's best fish glue and two ounces of grape sugar in five ounces of clean water. In another glass dissolve one-half ounce of ammonium bichromate in five ounces of clean water. When both are perfectly dissolved, pour the two solutions together, and stir them well, after which the mixture should be filtered several times.

These solutions should be prepared in the dark room and should not be kept more than a day or two, as both light and time will destroy their power. They should be kept in the dark room in a glass-stoppered bottle.

The sensitive solution, however it may have been made, should be poured over the clean, dry glass plate already described, as soon as possible after it is made. This is done in exactly the same manner that photographers prepare wet plates. The waste solution running off the glass plate should be filtered and saved as it may be used again. This pouring must be done in the dark room and dust must be carefully avoided. The wet plates should now be dried on an iron frame covered with paper and heated from underneath by a small gas or alcohol lamp. They should not be heated hotter than the hand can comfortably bear. When they are perfectly dry, they should be left in the dark room in a dry, warm place, free from dust and should be used the same day.

The next step is to place the negative that is to be reproduced in a copying frame with the glass side out. It should be perfectly clean and free from dust. The sensitive plate is then put in the frame with the sensitive side towards the negative. Any friction between the plates must be avoided. This, of course, is done in the dark room. The plates are now exposed in the sunlight from half a minute to a minute. If exposed in the shade it will take from five to ten minutes. If the weather is very damp it is advisable to use a previously warmed sensitive plate and negative for exposure to the light, since damp weather injures the sensitiveness of the plate. Also it is well to avoid any sudden change of temperature during the exposure. In the winter it is best to make the exposure in a warm room having about the same temperature as the dark room.

After the exposure is finished, the copying frame should be carried to the dark room, where the next operation must take place. First, the exposed sensitive plate should be taken carefully out of the copying frame and placed on a piece of paper with the sensitive side upward. The picture will not as yet be discernible upon it. Now place a quantity of black or brown dry enamel paint on the plate and gently scatter this powder over it by means of a soft, clean, dry brush, which should be kept for this purpose only. Then brush the enamel powder back into its bottle. It is very essential that no dust shall get into it. After five or ten minutes repeat the powdering and so on two or three times until the picture is clearly developed.

If the sensitive plate has been underexposed, the picture will develop rather quickly at the first powdering. This will generally give blurred reproductions, and it is scarcely worth while to bother longer with that plate. The only thing to do is to make another exposure. With a well exposed plate, the picture should develop slowly, that is, not before the second or third powdering. If the weather has been exceedingly dry, it is advisable to breathe gently on the exposed sensitive plate before beginning the powdering. If, on the other hand, the weather has been damp, the plate should be warmed slightly before powdering.

Fig. 11. Pickle Pot or Dip Basket.

When the picture shows clearly, brush all the surplus powder carefully from the plate, which is now ready to be treated with collodion. Add about twenty drops of castor oil to a pint of 2 per cent collodion solution and mix it thoroughly. This mixture, which must be free from air bubbles, should now be poured over the powdered plate. The waste collodion which runs off the plate is contaminated by traces of the enamel paint and cannot be used again. After the collodion has hardened, cut around the edges of the plate with a knife and then place the plate with the collodion side upward in a dish containing a weak solution of caustic potash (half an ounce of caustic potash dissolved in a quart of water). This solution will remove all the chromium which has served its purpose. Leave the plate in this solution until the first appearing yellow coloring has disappeared, and then place it with the collodion side upwards in a basin with slowly running water, which will in about an hour wash away all the chromium and potassium salts. The plate should then be placed in a dish of clean water to which a few drops of nitric acid have been added, not more than enough, however, to give the water a slight sour taste. The plate may remain over night in this solution without harm to the picture, although a couple of minutes will be found entirely sufficient if one is in a hurry.

Next, the plate should be placed in a large basin of clean water with the collodion side downwards. If the collodion film has previously been cut properly around the edges, it will soon separate from the plate, which may be removed, leaving the collodion film floating in the water.

Meanwhile, the enameled metal plate, which has been prepared exactly the same as is done for enamel painting, should be cleaned with a soda solution to free it from all grease. It should now be placed upon a wire support and carefully brought under the floating film which can be deposited gently on the enameled surface by means of a soft brush. The plate should then be taken slowly out of the water and the overlapping parts of the film should be turned under the edges of the plate, after which it should be put on a piece of white blotting paper to dry.

If any air bubbles appear under the film, they should be brushed very gently with a soft, wet brush towards the edge of the plate, where they will do no harm. If this does not prove successful, the bubbles may be opened with a needle, after which the air may be pressed out with a wad of soft paper.

When the plate with the collodion film on it is perfectly dry, the collodion should be removed by placing the plate in a dish of concentrated sulphuric acid. Within a few minutes the collodion will entirely dissolve. When this has taken place, a brownish ring will appear around the plate, whereupon the plate should be removed at once and put in a large basin of clean water. Finally, it should be submerged in a weak solution of ammonia (one ounce of ammonia to a quart of water), which will neutralize the last traces of the acid, after which it should be left on a piece of blotting paper to dry.

The picture may now be retouched just as photographers retouch ordinary photographs, only the same enamel paint should be used that was used in the powdering process. After the retouching, the plate may be fired in a muffle, just as is an ordinary enamel painting, and then covered with a layer of fondant. The finished photograph may, however, be painted with enamel paints if the enameler desires to make a colored photograph.

CONTENTS

PREFACE.. 3

INTRODUCTION 3

CHAPTER I   PREPARATION OF THE ENAMELS 6

CHAPTER II   PREPARATION OF THE METALS 9

CHAPTER III   CHARGING 12

CHAPTER IV   FIRING..17

CHAPTER V   STONING..20

CHAPTER VI   POLISHING...24

CHAPTER VII   FOILS—PAILLONS—GLITTER ENAMEL—DULL
FINISH—PLIQUE-À-JOUR 27

CHAPTER VIII   ENAMEL PAINTING 31

CHAPTER IX   PHOTOGRAPHS ON ENAMEL 35